Boarding the Plane with Tyler & Max

CLAUDIA TAN

Early morning sun

gentle breezes brush the pine

where little squirrels run

—Gwyn Dunham

TABLE OF CONTENTS

PLAYBILL...I

TYLER & MAX...V

Chapter 1
AIM HIGH 1

Chapter 2
MANHATTAN BOUND..4

Chapter 3
DISCOVERED 9

Chapter 4
THE SUBWAY 16

Chapter 5
CENTRAL PARK 22

Chapter 6
MAKING A LIST...45

Chapter 7
UP AND AWAY..50

Chapter 8
NIAGARA FALLS 72

Chapter 9
ANCHOR BAR/BUFFALO WINGS...............................94

Chapter 10
ON OUR WAY HOME..103

PHOTO GALLERY..117

PLAYBILL

 **Tyler**—Well read, analytical, and very protective of his twin brother Max. He is a planner and a doer. Detailed organizational skills and determination are Tyler's trademark. His keen sense of humor and tolerance guide him whenever he deals with Max's hijinks.

 **Max**—The lethargic twin who is content to let Tyler plan their daily activities and larger-than-life adventures. Max has a lively imagination and enjoys a good time as long as someone else puts in the hard work.

 **Aunt Julie**—Sophisticated and a meticulously groomed beauty, originally from New York City, has traveled extensively and has lived in Paris and Rome. Tyler and Max are her favorite nephews, who she counsels with her worldly wisdom. Max is infatuated with her collection of Japanese artwork and paintings.

 **Cousin Teddy**—A true intellectual and philosopher. While some may think of him as a loner, he is a cultivated and entertaining host. Teddy invited Tyler and Max to visit him in his neck of the woods, which meant they had to venture out of their sheltered neighborhood. It was a success and gave them the confidence to pursue new exploits.

Liam—A burly, brown-furred, in-charge leader of Madison drey. He is known for his cooking prowess and innovative recipes. On Saturdays, guests show up around dinnertime to join Liam for his aromatic roasted specialties. He is a tour guide extraordinaire and is delighted to show visitors his home turf, enchanting Central Park.

Chuckles—An educated, fun-loving member of the Madison drey. He is a history devotee and enjoys researching local trivia. On weekend evenings, Chuckles performs a spellbinding magic show— *Make It Disappear Chuckles*, which is always packed with members of the neighborhood dreys. Ginger is his loyal and stunningly-attractive girlfriend.

Ginger—A red-furred knock-out who attracts attention wherever she goes. Ginger is shy and enjoys being with her boyfriend Chuckles, who lifts her spirits and always provides a good laugh. Madison drey is home, but she keeps in contact with her sister, who lives in their hometown of Portland.

Carly—Enjoys music and early American poetry. From St. Louis, she is a well-known member of the Madison drey. On Sunday evenings, Carly can be found at the Loch reciting her fanciful poems. She has had many positive reviews in *Bright Artists*, a community newsletter. Visit her blog with over 800 members.

Leroy—He is a wise and respected leader of the Niagara drey who relishes the thought of tourists visiting his beloved Niagara Falls. Leroy is an older fellow but muscled and athletic. He is the go-to-guy for anyone seeking information on his electrifying city. If there's any kind of party in the neighborhood, Leroy will be there. Stan is his sidekick.

 **Stan**—Is affectionately known as the *Niagara buffoon* because of his witty and wacky antics. He is Leroy's best friend and a resident of Niagara drey. His long-time girlfriend lives in Binghamton. When she graduates in June, she will join his drey. Stan will give you the shirt off his back.

 **Justin**—Has been in show business for over ten years. He started his career as a male model. Justin is currently the spokesman for *Snazzy Dresser*. His gorgeous girlfriend Emmy will be in a magazine spread with him next month, a travel-log of Nova Scotia.

 **Emmy**—Is a fashion model who is well-known in Canada for her TV commercials. Her holiday calendars have sold millions of copies. She is black-furred, photogenic, and a talented actress. Look for Emmy in next season's *Ghosts from the Past*. She will be starring with her current boyfriend, Justin.

TYLER & MAX

Tyler and Max are warm-hearted spirited twin brothers who invite you to engage in a fact-finding mission with them, which will prove to be entertaining and informative.

An airplane ride to Buffalo and a bus ride to Niagara Falls are on the list. First, they'll make a stop in Manhattan to check out a few landmarks where they'll encounter some insightful and discerning characters. Little-known details emerge that will challenge and engage their senses.

Tyler is focused, and Max is eager to participate in the much-anticipated and long-planned endeavor. There will be some twists and turns along the way. Let's see how resourceful Tyler and Max are and how they prepare for the mini odyssey.

1
AIM HIGH

"We want to take a trip to Manhattan. How do we get there? We want to go on an airplane ride to Niagara Falls. How do we go about that?"

It's like a crossword puzzle; no matter how clever you think you are, sometimes you have to look up an answer. Tyler and Max have a lot to figure out. Pencils and a yellow pad are at their disposal for formulating a strategy. Their goal—a burning desire to take on the world!

TYLER

Join the celebration and observe the clever maneuvering. Nothing less than an ongoing rendezvous with discovery and adventure.

MAX

DECISIONS

"Max, tomorrow we're taking a trip to Manhattan. The way I see it, there are several ways to get there. We can take the subway, the Long Island Railroad, a bus, or an Uber."

"All the choices, Tyler—I'm a bit confused."

"Agreed, then let's do the easiest, Uber."

"But you need an app, Tyler, right? Don't you?"

"I've got that covered. I loaded the Uber app on my cell phone yesterday. Fortunately, Aunt Julie let me use her credit card. Uber wants a credit card. That's how the trips get paid."

"Aunt Julie is very accommodating and gracious, but when will we be employed and have our credit cards?"

"Soon. I know we will get jobs, Max, then we'll have our money and credit cards."

He shakes his head in agreement. "I hope so, Tyler."

"Max, about our excursion to Manhattan, I've looked at several brochures and think Paley Park will be first on our list."

"Paley Park?"

"Most people don't even know about it. It's a secluded park on 53rd Street. There's a high wall with a dazzling waterfall. Next, of course, would be Central Park. I know we can find some relatives there."

"Sounds like a plan, Tyler. Let's not forget our money belts and cell phones. I'm going to place them right by the divider. I want to wear my beret, and of course, we'll need our sunglasses."

"Good thinking. Now I suggest we get some sleep. Tomorrow will be a busy day."

2
MANHATTAN BOUND

Today was the big day; the weather was agreeable. Max texted for an Uber to Fifth Avenue and 53rd Street. Three minutes later, a shiny white SUV pulled up in front of the park, where they were waiting anxiously.

The driver stepped out of the car and asked, "Uber for Tyler and Max?"

"Yes, I'm Tyler, and we ordered an Uber to take us to Paley Park in Manhattan."

"Very good."

He opened the back door and assisted them. Once in, they buckled up and put on their prized sunglasses. It was mid-morning, and there was hardly any traffic. The Uber was heading to Manhattan; after several stops at traffic lights, the 59th Street Bridge was in sight.

Tyler leans over and tells Max, "The bridge we'll be crossing is also known as the Ed Koch Queensboro Bridge."

"Who is Ed Koch?"

"Ed Koch was the mayor of New York City in the 1980s."

"I have a feeling that we're going to learn a lot more history before our trip is over."

"You can count on that, Max."

"For now, let's look ahead and observe. See all the tall buildings?"

The driver inquires, "Is this your first trip to Manhattan?"

"It is. We're so excited," Max answers.

Second Avenue awaits them as they leave the bridge. Buses, blaring horns, and noise galore greet the twins.

"Now we're entering Manhattan. See the magnificent Art Deco building? That's the Chrysler Building, and the tall one is the Empire State Building. I would plan a visit. When you take an elevator and get to the top, you'll have a birds-eye view of the city."

"Tell us more."

"I would suggest the Metropolitan Museum of Art and Rockefeller Center."

"We'll keep those in mind."

Max asks, "Mr. Driver, how far to Paley Park from here?"

"Not too far, should be there in less than five minutes."

The Uber makes a left turn on 53rd Street.

"OK, you have arrived, Paley Park."

"Thank you, Mr. Driver. We enjoyed the ride and your recommendations."

"You're welcome. Enjoy the day."

Tyler opens the door and steps out of the car. Max follows. Seeing the waterfall, they are taken aback by its splendor and calm. Neither one moves until Max breaks the silence.

"How can such a waterfall exist in a busy city? I would never have expected it. Tyler, it's an oasis in the middle of a huge metropolis. Look, round tables and white wire chairs. Let's sit on the stone ledge by the quaint little restaurant."

"That would be a pleasant place to collect our thoughts and finalize our agenda."

They hop on the cement ledge, lean back, and observe the unruffled ambiance. Tyler takes a few Central Park photos from his jade-green waistband and shows them to Max. One is a picture of the charming Central Park Carousel; the other is a place known as the Mall.

"Max, did you ever see so many trees?"

Removing his sunglasses and taking a long look, "Not in one place, I haven't. The Mall looks like an umbrella of towering trees. I would like to ride one of the carousel horses. My imagination is running wild! I'd like to see it all, Tyler."

"We will. Let's enjoy Paley Park for a while."

3
DISCOVERED

As they sat on the ledge, the waterfall and its mesmerizing allure and serenity brought a sense of well-being. The air was fresh and nippy. A very handsome man in a khaki safari photo vest came up to where they were sitting. He had a giant camera, held on a thick black neck strap.

"Hello, my name is Otis Parson, and I noticed how distinguished you look."

Tyler and Max glance up.

Mr. Parson continues, "Your poise and posture set you apart from the crowd. What are you doing in Paley Park today?"

"Nice to meet you, Mr. Parson. My name is Tyler, and Max is my twin brother. We are thrilled to be here. You see, we are from Forest Hills and have been planning a trip to Manhattan for a long time."

"How do you like it?"

Tyler looks at Max and confirms, "We're enjoying ourselves. The ride over here was eye-opening. There's a lot more traffic in Manhattan than in Forest Hills and more high-rise buildings."

"Are the two of you in show business?"

"Why would you ask that, Mr. Parson?"

"I can see how everyone in the park is looking at you and admiring your demeanor and choice of accessories."

Tyler asks, "You mean Max's maroon beret and our sunglasses?"

"Absolutely, with all the attention you're garnering, everyone must think you're celebrities."

Max looks at Tyler, and they both grin ear to ear.

"Why thank you, we try to be trendy, but at the same time classy," Max responds.

"Are you employed now?"

Acting sophisticated, Tyler interjects, "Not at the moment, but we're open to all suggestions."

He asks them politely, "May I take your photo with the waterfall in the background?"

Max asks, very obligingly, "How should we pose?"

"Get close together and look to the left. I want to see your strong jawlines. The more natural, the better."

After examining the photo, Mr. Parson exclaims, "Well, the two of you are just what I'm looking for."

Crossing his arms, Max asks, "We are?"

"I could use you in some of our advertising campaigns. That would mean some travel and overnights in hotels. You would be promoting products for our customer base. Would you be interested in such a job? Naturally, the pay would be substantial."

"Not only would we be interested, but when would Max and I start?"

"Soon, here's my business card, Tyler. Think it over. I'll text or call you, and we'll arrange for some studio photos and promotional material if you're agreeable."

He hands Tyler a blank card, "Please write your phone number."

"Yes, sir, and thank you."

He writes his number and gives the card back to Mr. Parson.

"Tyler and Max, could I ask a favor?"

"Sure, what can we do for you?" Tyler inquires.

"Before I go, I'd like one more photo, without your sunglasses and Max's beret. Just your face, and please look straight ahead. I need your profiles."

Tyler and Max face each other and raise their chins ever so slightly.

Mr. Parson clicks away and shows them the photos.

"You made us look good, Mr. Parson." Max gleams.

"Well, thank you, I have a good eye for talent. I'm going to get a coffee and croissant, right here, at the French Bakery. I'm in a hurry, so I'll be eating on the run. Enjoy the rest of your time in Manhattan."

Max couldn't contain his enthusiasm. "Tyler, I can't believe it. Do you think he was really on the level?"

"We'll wait for his text. You know what it all means, don't you?"

"I think I do. Soon we'll be independent and have our credit cards. Let's just keep our fingers crossed and hope it all works out."

"I think it will, Max, but for now, how about some hot chocolate?"

"Sure, with extra whipped cream!"

Tyler walks into the cafe and returns with two hot chocolates. As they sip, Max asks inquisitively, "What's next on the itinerary?"

"Finding a subway that will take us to Central Park."

"Very well, let's go."

Finding a trash bin, they dispose of the empty paper cups.

CONVENIENCE STORE

After leaving Paley Park and walking a few blocks, something at a local convenience store catches Max's attention.

"Tyler, look at that man!"

"Which one?"

"The one standing next to the green shopping cart filled to the brim with what looks like plastic bags and old blankets."

"Wow, and his baggy grey pants are torn in the back. Max, he only has one shoe! His other foot has an ankle bandage. He must be homeless. Look, he's telling the man who's going into the store that he's hungry."

The man assures him, "Don't worry. I'll get you a slice of pizza."

Tyler then hears the homeless man say, "I'm lactose intolerant. I can't have anything with cheese."

"OK then, I'll get you something without dairy."

The homeless man smiles. Max looks perplexed.

Tyler offers clarification, "Lactose intolerant means the inability to digest anything with dairy. Cheese has milk."

"Oh, I see, the poor soul, not only is he without a home but can't eat cheese pizza."

After a few minutes, the man comes out of the convenience store with a bag of potato chips and hands it to the man waiting eagerly. He takes the chips, smiles, and thanks the charitable stranger.

4
THE SUBWAY

The mission now is to get to the famed Central Park.

Standing tall and adjusting his sunglasses, Tyler tells Max, "Now we'll take the subway to Central Park. We need to look for the **DOWNTOWN E,** then connect to the **UPTOWN 1**."

"Where do we find the subway? Where is it?"

"Let's ask."

Tyler approaches a girl in a pale blue jogging outfit.

"Excuse me, could you please tell us how to get to the nearest subway? We want to go to Central Park."

"You're in luck; there's a subway on the corner of Fifth and 53rd—straight ahead. Do you have a metro card?"

"We do."

"Then go down the subway stairs at Fifth Avenue," as she points to the entrance.

"Thank you. You've been very helpful."

"You're welcome. Enjoy the park."

"We will, thanks again."

Quickly, the two head to the subway station. After taking a set of stairs and reaching the turnstile, they swipe their metro cards. A steep escalator takes them to a platform where they wait for the **DOWNTOWN E.**

"Max, I looked at the subway map yesterday. We're right where we should be. We'll go to **34th Street,** then take the **UPTOWN 1.**"

"Whatever you say, Tyler."

Glancing around as trains zoom by, Tyler warns Max, "Cover your ears. It's very noisy!"

When the **DOWNTOWN E** stops, they get on board. In a few stops, they get off at **34th Street** and look for the **UPTOWN 1.**

"So many signs Tyler, **UPTOWN, DOWNTOWN, QUEENS, BROOKLYN** and all the letters—**D, E, F, G, M,** and numbers."

"Max, let's look for **UPTOWN 1**."

"I see the sign."

A musician sitting in a chair against the subway wall was playing the cello. Several stood and listened while a lady in a floral dress chats with the artist and wants to know the name of the beautiful song he is playing. He told her it is an aria from *Madame Butterfly*.

Max overhears and asks Tyler, "Who is Madame Butterfly?"

"I'm not sure, maybe an actress?"

As they wait for the train and listen to the cello, Tyler shares a few facts.

"The New York City Subway is the busiest U.S. rapid transit system—with almost 6 million riders on any given day."

"And Tyler, I bet you know when it was built?"

"I do, 1904. Here comes the **UPTOWN 1**. We'll get off at **59th Street**."

The train isn't jam-packed. Tyler and Max get two seats together. A bearded man wearing pink shorts is playing the trombone and singing "On the Road Again." Several riders applaud.

The musician takes his trombone and gets off at the next station. Some pretty girl in white boots and purple braided hair boards the train and sets up a music station. Everyone looks up as she takes the mic and sashays confidently up the aisle and starts singing, "Come See About Me."

Max nudges Tyler, "She's like a goddess in that dress, and those white boots are edgy. What a voice! Do you think she'll let me take a picture?"

"Show her your cell phone and point to it."

Max takes his cell phone and shows it to her. The songstress smiles back. He takes a picture.

"I got it, Tyler, see?"

"I like it. Now let's pay attention. We don't want to miss our stop."

Two young boys cheer her on. More cell phones come out, and many others take pictures and clap as she sings another song. After a few stops, a recording announces **59th Street**.

As Max and Tyler leave, the singer waves goodbye.

She yells, "My name is Giselle. Come see my show in the Village."

Tyler and Max smile and give the thumbs up.

Once off the train, a staircase takes them to the street, where an entrance to Central Park is in view.

5
CENTRAL PARK

Before entering, several friendly comrades see them and call out. A cocoa-colored in-charge leader approaches.

"Teddy texted us this morning and told us you might be coming over. We've been on the lookout for you. I'm Liam. Say hello to my friends, Chuckles, and his beautiful red-furred girlfriend, Ginger."

"Pleased to meet you. I'm Tyler, and Max is my twin brother."

Max looks around. Tyler explains how they took an Uber from Forest Hills to explore some Manhattan sights.

"Well, you came to one of the most world-renowned parks. You're now officially in Central Park, where you'll find an abundance of trees, scenic drives, and prominent landmarks."

Being a good host, Liam inquires, "Before we leave, would you like to rest up for a while? If not, are you ready to see Belvedere Castle? It's not too far from here."

In unison, "We're ready to go and see Belvedere right now."

BELVEDERE CASTLE

Liam tells Max proudly, "The Belvedere Castle, which draws one million annual visitors, was closed for a 15-month renovation. It overlooks Central Park's Turtle Pond and the Great Lawn."

Tyler also listens attentively to Liam's expose.

"Most visitors and tourists go to the Statue of Liberty or Empire State Building, but I wanted to show you an outstanding piece of Manhattan. Few know, Belvedere has been renovated and restored to all its richness and glory. Admission is free, open to all. Follow my path, jump and swing with me—I'll be your guide. Since we have so many trees, it will be a hop, skip, and a few jumps away."

A variety of majestic trees fill the landscape. They follow Liam's lead and jump on the nearest tree.

"I'll point out extra-special attractions as we venture forward. We won't have time to stop, but when you come back to Central Park for a visit, they'll be yours to explore."

Both nod their heads in agreement.

"On the immediate left is Strawberry Fields."

"Max glances and asks, "Do they grow strawberries here?"

"No, it's a memorial named after The Beatles' song 'Strawberry Fields Forever.' The Beatles were a singing group from the 1960s."

"Shortly, we'll be passing the Central Park Zoo. Although not grand in size, it has the popular Tisch Children's Zoo, which contains a petting zoo. You and Tyler would enjoy spending some leisure time here."

Looking down, Tyler cries out, "Look, Max, that showy creature is a Red Panda—it's written on the sign. The brown and white ones with markings—I don't know. I can't see the sign. Liam, do you know what they are?"

"Sure. Children love them—Domestic Goats."

"We're absolutely coming back to visit all the animals."

"I suggest you visit at feeding time; it's something to see!"

"Tyler, we will, right?"

"Yes, I'd like to watch."

Continuing, Liam points out another attraction.

"Wollman Rink is on your left, right in the heart of Manhattan. Most will agree—it's one of the most beautiful skating venues in the world. You can see amazing views of the New York City skyline. In the winter, Max, can you imagine yourself skating on Wollman Rink?"

"I don't know about that, Liam. I think I'd just like to watch the others having fun at the sport."

"Ahead is the London Plane Tree—right near the Reservoir, likely, Central Park's oldest tree. Chuckles, one of our drey mates you met, is a history enthusiast. He researched and found that it's well over 100 years old, more likely closer to 150. The London Plane drey, aptly named, has been home to many through the years, but the drey has moved."

"Dignified tree, Liam, where's the London Plane drey now?"

"Not too far from ours. I can understand why the members and their drey moved. The daily crowds wanting a photograph of the celebrated London Plane Tree, and the non-stop commotion, made for a raucous neighborhood."

"Not too good, Liam," Max comments.

"Bethesda Fountain is next, a distinct gem. We're going to take a break and gather a look. Max, I know you like taking pictures, so get out your cell phone."

"Yes, Liam, my brother is a photo buff."

Max shakes his head, confirming.

"You will enjoy *Angel of the Waters,* the iconic sculpture at the top."

"She's a beauty Liam," Tyler remarks starring at the masterpiece.

"What is the angel holding in her left hand, Liam?"

"Tyler, it's a lily, which is a symbol of the water's purity. The four cherub figures below represent Peace, Health, Purity, and Temperance."

"That's quite a list."

"Yes, it is, and Bethesda Fountain is one of the largest fountains in New York City."

"OK, Liam, I got my pictures."

"Now, onward, my friends."

Tyler and Max follow Liam.

Moving along past high bushes and rambling trees, Liam declares authoritatively, "When visiting Central Park, travelers from all over clamor to see the world-class Belvedere Castle. Well, here it is, in all its glory, what I promised—Belvedere!"

Looking at the stately edifice, Max tosses his head back for a better view.

"Can we go inside, Liam?"

"That's why you're here; I'll show you the spiritedness of Belvedere Castle."

"I'm a little nervous, Liam. It's huge and foreboding."

"Yes, Max, it sits atop Vista Rock, the second-highest natural elevation in Central Park."

Tyler is concerned; he knows about Max's initial trepidation to pursue something new.

He quietly tells Liam, "He likes to jump headfirst into new adventures, but at the same time becomes tense."

Liam acknowledges what he heard.

Quickly he asks Max, "What do you think about the troubadour playing the violin near the entrance to Belvedere?"

"I like the music and the colorful balloons surrounding him."

"I do, too. Let's enjoy the fresh air and listen to the violin.

It sounds like the song he's playing is 'Sweet Caroline.' A little out of tune—but enjoyable nonetheless."

Five minutes goes by; it gives Max time to calm his nerves.

"All right, Liam, I'm ready," as he takes a deep breath.

They proceed toward the lookout towers in a single file, which provides the best views. Liam stops and points out the scenic structures.

"Look ahead. You'll see Turtle Pond and the Great Lawn. They are two connected features of Central Park—located on a former reservoir for the Croton Aqueduct system. During the early 20th century, the Commissioner of Parks and Recreation, Robert Moses, ordered it drained and filled."

"How historic! I'm enjoying the information and stunning views," Max excitedly tells Liam.

"Then, how about this? The pond was originally known as Belvedere Lake. It is neighbors with Belvedere Castle and the Delacorte Theater and contains a variety of turtles and fish. The Great Lawn is composed of 14 acres of oval-shaped land."

After trying to register the facts, Tyler asks, "14 acres? What is the Great Lawn used for? Where do all the turtles come from?"

"I'll explain. The Great Lawn is mainly a recreational field. You can see an oval walkway surrounds it. There are baseball fields on the Great Lawn, as well as a soccer field and basketball courts."

"Impressive. What about Turtle Pond?"

"Turtle Pond is located south of the Lawn. Most of the parks' turtles live in Turtle Pond. It's thought that many are former pets people brought to the pond."

"How interesting."

"Another enhancement," he went on, "is that the windows and doors at the Castle were replaced with clear pane glass to improve visitors' sightlines."

"They went out of their way to make Belvedere Castle a premiere attraction."

"Yes, Tyler, it was quite an undertaking."

"And what about the Delacorte Theater?"

"The magnificent Delacorte Theater, which seats 1800, was also modernized."

"I can see it's an open-air theater, but what takes place there?"

"Staged productions of Shakespearean plays. The best part—it's free to the public."

"Max and I read *Hamlet*. I enjoyed the part about, 'To be, or not to be, that is the question.'"

"Tyler, then you and Max should come back next month. *Hamlet* will be playing for two weeks."

"Hear that, Max?"

"We'll surely be here, Liam."

"Excellent. You've just seen Belvedere; now I have a real treat for you—North Woods. It's not too far from here. Are you up for another park stunner?"

Max looks at Tyler for guidance.

"Liam, if it's not too much trouble. Max and I don't want to impose on you. You've already been very generous with your time."

"Not at all. I'm enjoying your company. I'll take you to North Woods. There you will see, in all its beauty—a treasured, inviting site, known as the Loch."

"What exactly is North Woods?" Max asks.

"North Woods, located in the park's northwestern section, is rugged woodland. Magical and nature at its finest. You won't even think you're in New York City. Dazzling waters are known as the Loch and the Pool, which will astound and entertain you."

"Liam, you say the Loch, but what exactly does that mean?"

"Max, *loch* is a Scottish word for lake."

"I get it—a lot of water."

"For sure, a restful, picturesque haven. Stone arches, bridges, and a bevy of flowers will engage your senses. At least four compact but graceful waterfalls are in the area if you can imagine that?"

"I see there are two paths. Which one are we going to take, Liam?"

"We'll continue on the sunnier one, Max," as he points ahead.

"I am looking forward to seeing another waterfall. You see, we saw one earlier today at Paley Park. The honey-like scent in the air is probably those flowers you mentioned."

"Well, Max, the flowers giving off the honey aroma are forsythias. And, right in front of you, here's another waterfall."

"Wow, it's not flowing from a wall like Paley."

"No, Max, it's not."

"Max, the waterfall races down over 14 feet of rocky edge into a flowing pool. Very alluring this time of year."

"Liam, it's dimly lit, restful, and not as busy as your end of the park. The sound of the wandering water is peaceful. Can we just sit here for a while?"

"Of course. Notice how the surrounding boulders and parade of commanding trees frame the waterfall, especially steadfast maples and honey locusts. Here's a fun note—the Loch attracts an artistic group of drey dwellers who are fast asleep now."

"I see why. Almost hidden and nestled in an elusive garden with plenty of time to ponder and be creative. From what I can observe, the Loch easily lends itself to that. What time does the artsy group make an appearance?"

"Max, after sundown, you'll hear jazz and see the Loch come alive. An immense range of artwork will be displayed, including photos, paintings, and stone carvings."

"We won't be able to see them today, but we'll head back here when we see *Hamlet*."

"I think it would be very worthwhile. And one final surprise, another cascade of water just ahead."

Tyler observes, "It is amazing how much diversity exists in the landscapes of Central Park. The pageantry of nature on display and lots to do and take in. Maybe it should be a village all by itself. I like the way birds are strategically perched throughout the trees and embrace the neighborhood."

"Many flying beauties make the park their home. I've seen owls, falcons, woodpeckers, hawks, and hummingbirds. You wouldn't believe the number of folks who come here on bird expeditions."

"Liam, we will come back and look for all the birds. We can even join an expedition."

Max is gazing at the next waterfall, looks up, and nods his head in the affirmative. The three sit on nearby bedrock and listen to the sounds of nature. Fresh lilacs overwhelm the air. Weeping willows drape over the Loch.

"Tyler, how is Teddy? I haven't had the pleasure of his company for many months. Tell him to join you for your next visit."

"He's living by himself. He prefers solitude, but he was quite the entertainer when we went to see him. He enjoys reading and exploring his community. We will ask him to come with us when we see *Hamlet*. A stop at your drey will be first on the list."

"I am looking forward to your return with Teddy."

He asks Max, "What are your impressions of Belvedere Castle, the Loch, and Central Park overall?"

"A lot of history, wondrous scenery, and what a wide range of topics you covered. I feel like I've spent a day in the country."

"Perfect, now we can return to where you first entered the park."

Max and Tyler stretch, catch their balance and follow Liam. Gliding through the massive entanglement of trees, they quickly arrive where it all began.

CAMP MADISON

"Before you leave for Forest Hills, I want to show you our drey, affectionately referred to as Camp Madison. I have chickpeas roasted in a spice mixture with meaty walnuts for you to nosh on."

Very quietly, Max asks Tyler, "What are roasted chickpeas—we never had them, have we? I wonder what that is."

Before Tyler can answer, Liam fills in, "Chickpeas are legumes, in the same family as peas and peanuts. They're also called garbanzo beans, a good source of protein and fiber. You'll need energy for your trek back home. I roast a pot every week. And the distinctive aroma from the spice I add fills the entire drey. A true favorite in Camp Madison."

"Sounds intriguing. I can't wait to try your special mix," Max exclaims.

"You'll enjoy it."

Liam stops at a rugged tree with wide branches.

"Here's Camp Madison—our humble drey. Hop up. The entrance is behind the second twisted branch. Follow me."

The drey is extensive and has several winding corridors. At the end of a long hall is a bamboo string curtain that secures Liam's area. Music is playing in the hallway.

"I know the music is loud. It's coming from Carly's section. She moved in a few weeks ago. Johnny Cash and Willie Nelson are her favorites. Carly is from Missouri. Last spring, she visited New York City with a classmate, fell in love with Central Park, and decided not to go back home."

Max asks, "How did she learn about Camp Madison?"

"One day, when we were all outside the tree, she saw us and struck up a conversation. One thing led to another, and before long, Carly called Camp Madison home."

"Jon isn't home now. He's from Quebec and also decided to live here. He was only supposed to be here for a few weeks. It's been well over two years since he joined the drey."

Tyler observes, "It's an international community, right here."

"Without a doubt. The only rules are lights out at 10 p.m., no loud parties, and a clean drey."

Liam passes through the bamboo curtain and leads Tyler and Max into his spacious sector. There are cobblestones scattered around the floor and several wooden benches. Brown linen cloth separates the rooms, and there is what looks like a makeshift table.

Max asks, "How long have you been here? I like the arrangement."

"Three years next month. My original drey was in downtown Washington Square. I decided to explore the city a little more. When I saw Central Park and the glorious trees, I knew it was for me."

"And how did you discover Camp Madison?"

"Max, it was meant to be. Curtis, a former resident gathering fruit outside, began talking to me and found out my drey was in Washington Square.

He then asked if I would be interested in living in Camp Madison. An empty section was available. Curtis could sense my strong interest. Before I knew it, I was getting a top-to-bottom tour, and that evening I moved into Camp Madison."

"That was an exciting story, Liam. There is a never-ending backyard of trees in Central Park and remarkable landmarks."

"Remarkable—yes. Max, here, have some of my homemade chickpea and walnut mix."

A plastic bowl, filled to the brim, is placed on the wood table.

"What a delicacy, Liam—delicious!"

The snacks were gone in a flash.

"Before we leave, I want to thank you for your time and lavish hospitality. Max and I have thoroughly enjoyed our visit to Manhattan. You were the best tour guide! Someday you'll have to visit us in Forest Hills."

"I would be delighted."

"Max, it's time to call an Uber."

Both waved goodbye to Liam as they left Camp Madison, then continued toward Fifth Avenue to wait for their ride. Immediately, a black Lincoln Continental pulled up to the curb.

OBSERVATIONS

The driver opened the door and welcomed them aboard. Before long, they were approaching the 59th Street Bridge.

"I know the other name for the bridge, Tyler. It's the Ed Koch Bridge. You told me this morning, and I remembered."

"Yes, and who was Ed Koch?"

"He was a former mayor of New York City."

Tyler smiled. He and Max leaned back, observed activities on Queens Boulevard, and made some perceptive observations.

"Tyler, I think we witnessed a considerable amount of goodwill in Manhattan today. And, the music seemed to be everywhere. We enjoyed many talented artists and singers. We have to make it a point to see Giselle perform in the Village someday.

I've heard many negative things, but boy, everyone we met was friendly and more than willing to help us."

"You can sure say that, Max, starting with our first driver and ending with our new-found friend Liam."

"Liam knew a lot, didn't he, Tyler? I enjoyed the savory treat he made for us. The combination of chickpeas and the special spice was tangy. I hope we will be able to return to Central Park and visit the other sights Liam pointed out."

"For sure, Max. I, too, was moved by the compassionate man, who bought the vagrant a bite to eat. It was an uplifting experience. I assure you, we will visit Giselle soon. I enjoyed her singing."

The driver let them off in front of the schoolyard.

It started to rain as they crawled up the tree. The ragged sock, which acted as a door, was pushed aside as Tyler and Max made their grand entrance. Not much was said, as they were still absorbing the events of the day.

Tomorrow would be time enough for a new direction—an innovative strategy.

6
MAKING A LIST

The morning sun illuminated the drey. Max had finished his first cup of coffee and a handful of raw cashews.

"Tyler, we've had two very successful jaunts; the visit with Teddy last year and our recent trip to Manhattan. I think we can start making plans for our next adventure—an airplane ride. How do you think we should go about it?"

"I've been giving it some serious consideration. Always make a list. That's what Aunt Julie advised me to do when making an important decision. A yellow pad works. Draw a line down the middle of the page—pros on one side and cons on the other. I'll show you what I've come up with. Here's what I put together."

He picks up a yellow pad in the corner.

"For our trip, we've been talking about going to Niagara Falls. I can't wait to hear your proposals."

"OK, Max, here are some pros. Our trip will be a mini-vacation. We'll make new friends and see new places. We need some fun, and an airplane ride will surely broaden our horizons."

"I like what I'm hearing."

"We will need plane tickets to Buffalo. I checked out all the airlines and decided on American Airlines."

"Tyler, I see you did your usual research. Why American Airlines and why Buffalo? What makes American Airlines special?"

"For starters, American Airlines is the largest airline in the world! I saw their extensive route map, which showed hundreds of destinations. As for Buffalo, it's less than an hour to Niagara Falls by car. There's transportation to the Falls once we land."

"Another Uber, Tyler"

"No, I've been on the tourist website. On the day we're going to Buffalo, a chartered bus will take us to Niagara Falls. The bus leaves a few hours after we land. I spoke with a representative from the tour company and got us a good deal."

"Sounds sort of complicated but exciting at the same time. And what about the cons, Tyler? What's on the list?"

"Only one. Yes, it's a challenge, and maybe there are some risks. However, if we don't go, we'll be missing out on an experience of a lifetime."

"When we crossed Austin Street for the first time, we felt anxious. But, once we successfully got to the other side, we knew we could accomplish whatever we put our minds to."

"You convinced me, Tyler. Now, where do we get our tickets, and what do we need to pack?"

"Good questions. Niagara Falls is on both the U.S. side and the Canadian side. With that in mind, we will need a passport to get into Canada."

"How do we get a passport?"

"I found out two passport size photos and our birth certificates are needed. We can either go to a passport office or post office with our application, documentation, and a fee. In a few weeks, we'll have our passports."

"That's quite a process, Tyler."

"Yes, but well worth it. And, the passport is good for ten years."

"Two questions, where do we get passport applications? Where do we get photos?"

"Applications are available at the post office, right here in Forest Hills. There's a camera shop specializing in passport photos on Austin Street."

"Tyler, I think I understand the process for the passport. But, what about our plane tickets to Buffalo? Where do we get them?"

"Round-the-World Travel is a few blocks from here—that would be a good place to ask questions and get our tickets since we're new at this."

"Let's get going. I suggest passport photos first, then a stop at the travel agency."

"Perfect, Max. Let's fix ourselves up and head over to Austin Street."

They submitted their completed applications to the Forest Hills Post Office with their birth certificates, required photos, and full payment. Aunt Julie knew how excited Max was about the trip to Buffalo. She paid the extra *Rush My Passport* fee to have their passports sent in an expedited manner.

The next day, Tyler and Max visit a local travel agency, which was very receptive to their inquiry. A sales clerk issued one-way tickets for their trip to Buffalo from LaGuardia airport. Two airline codes made their appearance—LGA and BUF.

Amtrak is their choice for the return trip back to Forest Hills. That way, New York State could be seen up-close and personal.

"Max, I think we better go home and decide what we need to pack for our trip. It's starting to get dark, and we're leaving for Buffalo tomorrow."

"I would think the fewer items in our backpack, the better. Let's keep it light."

"I agree. The passports that arrived today, and plane tickets for sure."

"We have to pack the folding pillows from Aunt Julie. I'm taking my sunglasses and wearing my beret."

"Max, sunglasses, of course. We'll need our waistband belts for cell phones and credit cards."

"Sounds good. If we forget or need anything, we can buy it as we go along."

"Yes, I'm sure there are plenty of stores in Buffalo and Niagara Falls."

7

UP AND AWAY

After getting out of the Uber and looking for an entrance to American Airlines, Max sees a sliding glass door. Passengers are walking through with garment bags and suitcases. Max leads the way.

"Follow me, Tyler."

Check-in counters and screen monitors are in view when they pass through the door. A security area, where passengers line up to get screened, is visible.

"Now, what do we do, Tyler?"

"Just like we planned, we have to go through security. The machines you see are kind of like the ones in the library. They are looking for metal or devices. We'll put our backpacks on the moving belt. Then we wait for them to pass through."

"Yes, but first, let's find out what gate we're at. I see that the flights are in alphabetical order."

"Good starting point, Max."

Both look at the monitor for their gate.

"Tyler, I see it. **Flight 467 to Buffalo—Gate D8.**"

"**D8,** got it."

"Max, what a modern airport. Look around, look up, and look at the walls. Did you ever see so many inviting shops and artistic exhibits? It's a new airport. I read about it. Supposed to be the best one in the States now."

"I can see why."

THE SECURITY CHALLENGE

Fortunately, there are only a few passengers ahead of them. Max and Tyler place the backpacks carefully on the conveyer belt and are now at the front of the security line.

A TSA worker signals for the two to walk through the X-ray scanner. "One at a time," she cautions.

Tyler goes first. Max observes.

"You're next. Proceed slowly," as she waves him forward.

Max walks cautiously through the monitored area. When he gets to the end, he grabs Tyler's arm and is relieved.

Soon, a voice calls out, "Don't forget your backpacks and belts."

They retrieve their backpacks, put on the belts, and take an escalator to the gates.

"That was quite a process, Tyler, but we must have done everything right—because now we're in a secure area looking for **Gate D8**."

"You did well, Max. How about the corner display, see all the souvenirs? When we get to Buffalo, I bet they have some at their airport. I made a list; we'll need at least five local souvenirs. Niagara Falls will have plenty."

"Tyler, you're always planning. Nothing is left to chance with you."

"Speaking about chance, there's **Gate D6**. Only two more until ours. Let's stop for a while at the colorful fountain, with the changing shapes and impressions."

"Tyler, the Statue of Liberty, is encased in a waterfall of lights."

"And, the images are transforming right in front of our eyes. It's picture time, Max."

Max takes a quick photo, and the two proceed through the concourse.

"I'm not hungry, but there are quite a few restaurants in the D concourse. Smells like caramel, coffee, and toast all rolled into one."

"It does. I'm too excited to eat, and here's **Gate D8**. I see a plane parked at the gate. It must be ours, don't you think so, Tyler?"

"I believe it is."

THE GATE AGENT

At **Gate D8**, they see a screen listing their flight number and destination—**Flight 467 Buffalo**. An agent greets them as they walk up to the podium. Tyler notices the name on his navy blazer, Gary.

"Good afternoon. How may I help you today?"

Max hands the boarding passes to the agent and asks, "Gary, what else do we need to board the flight?"

Looking at the passes, he smiles and tells them, "Mr. Tyler and Mr. Max, you're all set. Have a seat in the boarding area, and when we call your group number, you can board."

"Could you please tell us what group we're in?"

"You're in **Group 2**," as he points out the group number on the boarding pass.

"Thank you, Gary. We appreciate your help."

"You're more than welcome. Enjoy the flight."

Tyler and Max find seats near the flight screen. Holding their boarding passes and watching other passengers check in with the agent, they relax.

Before long, Gary makes an announcement, "We will soon be boarding **Flight 467** to Buffalo. Please have your boarding pass available for inspection and wait for your group number to be called. Make sure you have all your belongings with you."

"That was quick, Tyler. It seems like we just got here. We've talked about this for a long time; now, our big moment is here."

"I know, but let's listen. We're in Group 2."

Another gate agent welcomed and called First Class passengers to board, then some select groups. When hearing their group called, passengers lined up at the boarding door. The gate agent scanned their passes and let them go through the jet bridge, which is a passageway that extends to the airplane.

Gary then made the following announcement. "The plane is now available for **Group 2** to board."

Tyler and Max jumped off the seats, took their backpacks, and went to the gate. Gary scanned their boarding passes and told them to have a fun trip. Smiling, they began walking down the jet bridge to the plane.

FLIGHT ATTENDANT GREETING

A flight attendant in a navy blue dress and sporting a fancy multi-color scarf greets them as they enter the plane.

"Good afternoon, welcome aboard. I see you have your boarding passes. Do you know where your seats are?"

Both answer, "No, we don't. This is our very first flight."

"OK then, you're in seats 33D and 33F. You have to pass through First Class, then continue straight ahead, and your seats will be on the left. Willie or Garnet will help you. But wait, since it's your first flight, how would you like to meet the captain?"

Not thinking he hears correctly, Max asks, "The captain of our flight?"

"Yes, Captain Duke Drake and First Officer Nora Ronstadt."

"Oh boy, we'd like that."

"My name is Shaylyn, and I'm working with Andy today."

MEETING THE CAPTAIN AND FIRST OFFICER

Shaylyn steps near the flight deck door and tells Captain Drake that twin brothers would like to visit.

"Sure, send them in."

Max and Tyler sheepishly saunter in to meet the captain.

"Come on up, I'm Captain Duke, and meet my First Officer, Nora."

"Pleased to meet you, I'm Tyler, and this is my brother Max."

"So, I hear this is your first trip?"

Looking around at all the switches and buttons, they were overwhelmed and couldn't answer.

"The weather is good from here to Buffalo. Do you have family there, or are you going to see Niagara Falls and get some Buffalo wings at the Anchor Bar?"

Answering very slowly, Tyler proclaims, "We have some friends, and we'll go along with what they have planned. I know for sure, Niagara Falls is on the list."

Smiling, "You'll enjoy the flight today and whatever you decide to do up in Buffalo."

"Thank you for inviting us. Wait until we tell our friends!"

Shaylyn escorted them out of the flight deck and told them their seat assignments. "Do you remember that, Tyler?"

"Yes, seats 33D and 33F. And one more time, where are they?"

"Go straight ahead. You'll pass through First Class and enter Main Cabin. Your seats will be on the left. Numbers and letters are above the seats. Since the flight isn't full, you'll have a seat between you for more comfort."

"Thanks, Shaylyn."

FIRST CLASS

Carrying their backpacks and strolling through First Class, they observed passengers seated and enjoying a beverage.

"Do you think we'll get a drink when we get to our seats, Tyler?"

"We're in Main Cabin, so I don't know. First Class customers get more amenities."

OUR SEATS

Now in Main Cabin, Max observes that the seats aren't as large as the ones in First Class. Shaylyn told them the numbers and letters are above, and Tyler points them out to Max.

"I see row 10; we have a way to go, all the way to row 33."

After passing the emergency exit and noticing supplies in some overhead bins, the two continue observantly to Row 33.

"Do you want the window or aisle seat? Remember, Shaylyn told us we'd have a seat between us?"

"I'd like a window seat, Tyler, so I can see what's happening."

"Good choice. There's another plane at the next gate. Wonder what city it's going to?"

Max takes his seat at the window and sets his backpack on the empty center seat. Tyler settles in and places his underneath the seat.

GAZING OUT THE WINDOW/LOADING LUGGAGE

"I'm seeing all the luggage being hoisted onto the conveyor belt and loaded into the plane. Quite an operation. The bags look heavy, but the ramp workers have no problem lifting them, Tyler."

ANNOUNCEMENT

"What do you think is next?"

Just as Max asked, a recorded message came over the loudspeaker.

Good afternoon. Welcome aboard American Airlines **Flight 467**, non-stop to Buffalo. Please place your carry-on items in an overhead bin or under the seat in front of you. If you need assistance, please let a flight attendant know.

If you are sitting in an emergency exit, please review the Safety Card in the seat pocket. You may need to open it in case of an emergency. Let a flight attendant know if you are unwilling to operate the exit or do not meet the exit seat requirements.

"Glad we're not sitting in an emergency exit."

"We're too young, Max. I read you have to be at least 15-years old."

More passengers were boarding, and the overhead bins were filling up. A flight attendant was closing them as she walked through the aisle.

"What attractive uniforms the flight attendants are wearing, Tyler. All look sharp and pulled together. Their scarves and ties have colorful designs. I overheard Garnet having a conversation with the girls sitting two rows up from us, saying that the Lands' End uniforms were new—and they've been wearing them less than a year."

Passengers were all seated when they heard the following announcement.

"Boarding is now complete. Flight attendants secure the cabin for departure."

Willie, the flight attendant, working the galley in the back, helped close the rest of the overhead bins and made sure all passengers were seated.

Shaylyn held the microphone and made the following address, "The forward door is now closed. Flight attendants arm doors and cross-check. Stand by for all call."

Max and Tyler were seemingly in their element and well on the way to becoming world travelers. With eyes wide open and observing every action, all was within their reach.

Soon, a recorded message would play. An announcement, which the two travelers would hear, many times over in the future.

Your safety is important to us. Please pause for a moment and give your full attention to the screens located throughout the cabin.

Tyler and Max sat up straight and watched attentively.

It was a long message. Passengers were told:

- to stow luggage, close tray tables, and place seats in the upright position.

- to fasten seatbelts (and how to do it).

- to comply with lighted and posted signs and crew instructions.

- all flights are non-smoking.

- to follow along with the Safety Card, which explains all the airplane's safety features.

- all exits are clearly marked with signs and opening instructions.

- if needed, exit path lighting will illuminate on or near the floor to guide you to an exit.

Tyler reaches for the Safety Card in the seatback pocket and follows along. Max does the same.

-if needed, a panel above your seat containing oxygen masks will drop down from an overhead compartment. Remain seated with your seatbelt fastened and pull the mask down to start the flow of oxygen. Place the mask over your nose and mouth and put the elastic band over your head. Pull the straps to tighten and breathe normally. Put on your mask before helping others.

-your life vest is in a compartment under or next to your seat. Pull the red strap to remove the life vest pouch. Take the vest out as shown on the Safety Card and put it over your head. Wrap the strap around the waist, attach the buckle, and tighten. Inflate your vest as you leave the airplane by pulling down on the red tab or by blowing into the red tubes. Never inflate the vest inside the airplane.

We will be dimming the cabin lights for takeoff. Individual reading light controls are overhead. Thank you for your attention. Enjoy your flight.

Max looked at Tyler. He put the Safety Card back into the seat pocket and commented, "That was quite a bit of information, but after seeing the video, it makes sense."

Willie and Garnet, who work in Main Cabin, came through after the video to do the safety checks. When passing by their row, Garnet tells Max that he has to put his backpack underneath the seat. He immediately complies.

A TARMAC DELAY

After everyone is seated, luggage stowed, and all flight attendants are in their assigned jump seats, a clear voice comes over the intercom.

"This is Captain Duke. It's another busy day at LaGuardia, especially in the early afternoon. First Officer Nora just spoke with air traffic control, and ATC informed us that we would have a delay of approximately 10 minutes before we can takeoff. We still anticipate an on-time arrival in Buffalo."

In less than five minutes American Airlines, **Flight 467,** was roaring down the runway.

AWAY WE GO

Tyler and Max sat up and made sure their seatbelts were securely fastened. It was a little bumpy speeding down the runway. As the plane lifted off the ground, relief, then amazement set in. They were soaring through the air. Max peered out the little window—the clouds looked like massive cotton figurines.

Five minutes into the flight, a chime is heard. Willie made an announcement.

"Once again, good afternoon. We have leveled off, and shortly we will begin our inflight service. We offer a selection of complimentary beverages. Our snack service includes pretzels or gingerbread cookies, which are also complimentary."

THE BEVERAGE SERVICE

Willie and Garnet begin pushing a well-stocked cart up the aisle from the aircraft's aft section. When the cart reaches their row, Garnet leans over and releases their tray tables.

"Thank you, Garnet. We didn't know how to use them."

"That's OK, Tyler, it's your first flight. Next time you'll be a real pro. Now, what would you like to drink?"

"Maybe, just a cup of water, Max, and I will share it."

"And would you like pretzels or cookies?"

"Pretzels for me. Max, would you like cookies?"

"No, Tyler, I'll just have a few of your pretzels."

"Only one bag of pretzels, please."

Garnet places a cup of water on Tyler's tray table and hands him a bag of pretzels.

"Thank you, Garnet."

"You're more than welcome. Just let me know if you or Max need anything else."

Tyler takes a few sips of water and then hands the cup to Max. Cloud formations captivate them. Max and Tyler enjoy the pretzels.

BUCKLE UP; WE'RE LANDING

After finishing the bag of pretzels, there is another announcement.

We are on our final approach to Buffalo. Please make sure your seatbelts are securely fastened, drop-down tray tables stowed, and seatbacks are in the full upright position. The flight attendants will be coming through the cabin one last time to collect any items you may wish to dispose of. We'll be on the ground shortly.

Willie and Garnet are coming through the aisle, collecting all service items. They check that all seatbacks are in the upright position, tray tables stowed, and seatbelts fastened. Willie stops at their row and addresses Tyler.

"It's your first flight, and here are two sets of wings. Captain Duke also signed a Junior Aviator Logbook for you. It's a keepsake. And, don't forget to fill out the applications for our frequent flyer bonus program. You can earn miles for today's flight and all your future flights on American Airlines."

Thoroughly surprised by the thoughtful gesture, he beams.

"Willie, thank you so much—we will always remember our first flight on American Airlines. I'll put the logbook and applications in my backpack right now—wow!"

The flight attendants returned to their jumpseats; Willie dimmed the cabin lights. Max continued to look out the window. It was such a smooth landing that Max and Tyler didn't realize that American Airlines **Flight 467** had landed at Buffalo Niagara International Airport.

TAXIING IN

Sitting upright with their seatbelts fastened, Tyler and Max listen to the last recorded announcement.

Welcome to Buffalo. Please remain seated with your seatbelt fastened until the seatbelt sign is turned off. Keep the aisles clear of all carry-on items.

Check your seatback pocket for any personal items, like tablets and cell phones. Please be careful when opening the overhead bins as items may have shifted in flight.

The Flight Attendant, who they met when boarding, makes a final public address.

"The local time is 2:10 p.m. American Airlines and our **one**world partners' thank you for flying with us today. On behalf of your New York and Dallas crew—we hope to see you again on another American Airlines flight. Have a wonderful day!"

"We made it, Tyler. We're here in Buffalo safe and sound."

"Yes, Max, what a pleasant flight, and the flight attendants were professional and friendly. And I enjoyed the captain's commentary. He kept us informed."

Max and Tyler reach under their seats for the backpacks. Passengers gathered their belongings from the overhead bins and moved steadily toward the front of the plane. Willie and Garnet were standing behind them and said goodbye to the two travelers. Max and Tyler thanked them and headed up the aisle toward the exit.

Before deplaning, they peek into the flight deck and thank Captain Duke and First Officer Nora. The captain said he hopes to see them soon on another American Airlines flight. Shaylyn and Andy extended their wishes for a safe and happy vacation.

They smiled and thanked the two flight attendants for an unforgettable flight.

Now, serious and focused, their goal was to find the tourist bus to Niagara Falls. When they reach the door at the top of the jet bridge, Tyler approaches the gate agent and asks where to find the bus to Niagara Falls.

Greg, who was checking in passengers for the flight back to LaGuardia, tells them to go down the escalator to the lower level, and the bus will be there.

Tyler thanks Greg and finds the sign, which directs them to the lower level.

"I see the sign, Max. Let's go. The bus departs at 4 p.m."

When they reach the lower level, a line has formed for the bus to Niagara Falls. Tyler and Max take out their tickets and join the group. The front door of the bus opens, and all start boarding. Max sees two seats together in the middle, and they get comfortable.

Little squirrel running

Climb up! scamper and scurry!

No time for pictures?

Tell me, what is your hurry?

—Gwyn Dunham

8
NIAGARA FALLS

Promptly at four o'clock, the door closes, and they're off.

"I enjoyed our airplane ride. I'm enjoying our bus ride, Tyler."

"Oh yeah, me too! For now, we can sit back and relax."

In less than 30 minutes, Max sees a sign —

NIAGARA FALLS 3 miles.

"We're almost there. It's my dream come true, Tyler!"

The bus stops abruptly, and the illustrious Falls are moments away. The driver picks up a microphone and makes an announcement.

"Welcome to Niagara Falls State Park, the oldest state park in the United States. In 2020, we celebrated its 135th birthday. There are three distinct falls—American, Bridal Veil, and Horseshoe Falls. All captivating in their own right.

There are many attractions—the Niagara Scenic Trolley makes six stops, which will acquaint you with the park's layout and history. If you plan on riding Maid of the Mist, be reminded it's only available on the American side.

Take an information handout as you leave and enjoy Niagara Falls and all it has to offer. Be careful when getting off the bus."

Arranging their backpacks, they make their way to the front of the bus. Everyone is chatting and moving quickly.

Tyler takes a brochure and proclaims excitedly, "Thank you, Mr. Bus Driver, you gave us a lot of good suggestions."

"You're welcome."

IT ROARS AND TANTALIZES

Safely off the bus, Max asks, "What's that loud noise?"

"It is loud, isn't it? Let's find out."

Reading the signs, they walk toward the tourist attractions. The sound becomes louder and louder.

"It's the rapids, Max, says right here in the handout."

"Mystery solved, but what are the rapids, Tyler?"

"It's the part of a river, which runs swiftly and wildly."

"Let's get closer and take a look."

They make their way toward the protective rails.

The view is water bouncing around, twisting, and moving incredibly fast, somehow flowing to the Falls.

"The noise, Tyler! I don't know how to explain what I'm hearing. Unless you've been here, there's no way to describe the roaring sound. It's startling and chilling!"

Tyler, slowly wandering toward the rails and getting closer to the rapids, observes a sign pointing to Niagara Falls.

"Let's follow it. Listen, Max, it's getting louder if that's even possible."

The trail leads to the boisterous American Falls.

In a few minutes, Max and Tyler stop in their tracks. Thunderous water is barreling over the Falls.

Neither can move. All they can do is stare. Max is uneasy.

Tyler suggests, "Close your eyes, breathe, Max, breathe. Smell the freshness of the mist!"

MAKING FRIENDS

It's not long before two hardy city fellows approach them. The older muscled one looks at Tyler, and in a low-pitched voice, greets him.

"Me and my buddy were watching you get off the tourist bus. Guess you're not from around here? If you need some help, we'd be glad to offer any assistance you might need."

Tyler and Max introduce themselves.

"I'm Tyler, and Max is my brother. We just got here from New York City. We live in Forest Hills."

"Big City folks."

"Not really. Forest Hills is more like a village."

"I'm Leroy, meet Stan. I'd like to make a suggestion before you start adventuring around. Why not put your backpacks in our drey? You can stay with us while you're visiting. That's if you don't have other plans."

"That would be convenient. Thank you, we're quiet and won't bother anyone," Tyler replies.

"It's the red oak tree near the Niagara Falls State Park welcome sign. You can't miss it. By the way, we're the Niagara drey."

They follow Leroy and Stan up the tree to the drey. Inside, Leroy gives a few bits of information.

"The small cove ahead is where you can leave your backpacks. To the left is a long narrow hall, a good place for some shut-eye. Next to the back door is a pantry, which Stan keeps well stocked. Feel free to help yourself."

"Thank you, Leroy and Stan. Your drey has a unique style. Max and I will enjoy spending some time here."

"We'll let you settle in. I suggest you walk around the park and then decide what sites you'd like to visit."

"Max took a brochure, which has the major attractions highlighted. But for now, we'll just walk around."

"Stan and I have a party to attend, at the Parkwood drey, around the corner. I'll leave you guys to explore, and we'll talk later or tomorrow."

"Thanks, Max and I will have plenty of questions."

After they stowed the backpacks, Max stuck the brochure in his red checked waist belt. Tyler and Max hurry down the tree and head back to Niagara Falls.

MAID OF THE MIST

Once on the ground, Max takes out the leaflet.

"Tyler, look at what it says about Maid of the Mist." Max hands it to Tyler, who reads aloud.

"Embark on a breathtaking tour on the world-famous Maid of the Mist boat cruise. Aboard the vessel, you'll catch the sight of Niagara Falls like never before. Venture into the heart of the awe-inspiring Horseshoe Falls, which is also known as Canadian Falls. Feel the mist on your face as 700,000 gallons of water hurtles over the Falls. It's a 30-minute seasonal boat ride up close to one of the Wonders of the World."

"Sounds like we have to go for it."

Pointing to the base of the Falls, Max says excitedly, "Look, I see Maid of the Mist, filled with tourists wearing some kind of blue covering. Of course, we'll experience everything, the mist coming off Niagara Falls and all its might. Just wait until we tell Teddy!"

"Here's more, Max."

"Afterwards, climb the steps of the Crow's Nest and get within feet of the American Falls. Watch the amazing power. Go up to the Observation Deck and take in the striking sight of all three Falls—a once-in-a-lifetime photo opportunity awaits. Next, visit Prospect Point, home to the Visitor Center, Niagara Adventure Theater, and Maid of the Mist. Learn about the daredevils who risked their lives for fame and glory—some succeeding and some succumbing to the might of Niagara."

"Tyler, there are so many enticing prospects. I don't know how we can see everything. Maid of the Mist got my attention. When are we going to take the boat ride?"

"Tomorrow, if it's sunny and warm. For now, let's just look at the wild teeming water."

THE FAMOUS BOAT

Waking up at the crack of dawn, Tyler and Max go to the Visitor Center to buy tickets for Maid of the Mist. A hearty breakfast and several cups of coffee give them the energy to take on the day. Having gotten up early and with tickets in hand allowed them to be first in line for the 9 a.m. boat ride. They were waiting at the Observation Tower's base at Prospect Point, where the famed flat-bottom boat embarks.

At 8:45 a.m., a crew member in a beige uniform begins collecting the tickets for the iconic voyage.

"Welcome, welcome! Take a poncho—you'll need it. Since it's the first Maid of the Mist ride today, you'll have plenty of room to spread out and take in the resplendent views of Niagara Falls. As we like to say, 'Direct and at close range.'"

Tyler and Max don the blue plastic ponchos and walk the plank, which leads to Maid of the Mist. A worker helps them step onto the boat. Before they were entirely situated and aware of what was happening, the boat sped off with a jolt.

As the boat chugged toward Niagara Falls, passengers were awed by the spectacle. All around the deck, loud *oohs* and *aahs* were heard. Sheer enjoyment and smiles were visible on the tourists' faces. Some tried to take pictures, but it was bouncy.

"We're rocking and rolling now, Tyler."

"We are. The ponchos aren't helping much. I'm soaked."

"Me too."

The tour guide grabs the mic and gives area facts and statistics as the boat gets closer and closer to the crashing waters.

"We're taking a journey into the heart of the mighty American and Horseshoe Falls. Hear the roar of 700,000 gallons of water falling right before your eyes. Feel the rush of the mist on your face.

Maid of the Mist tour has been running since the 1840s with a brief hiatus for the Civil War. It's North America's oldest tourist attraction; the operation has stayed nearly the same over the years except for the transition from steam to diesel. We've had some famous passengers, including Marilyn Monroe, Prince William & Diana, and Brad Pitt.

In a few minutes, Maid of the Mist will turn around and head back to shore. I won't make any more announcements. Enjoy the rest of the ride."

Max closed his eyes and held on tightly to Tyler. Very skillfully, Maid turned around and headed back to the dock. The celebrated American and Horseshoe Falls were behind them, and the ride was less turbulent. Before they knew it, the tour operator was assisting them off the boat.

"Tyler, Maid of the Mist, was such a thunderous ride. I enjoyed getting so close to the plunging water—it's magnificent but terrifying at the same time. Not for the faint of heart!"

"I guess we can truly say there's no better way to experience Niagara Falls."

"I don't know. Cave of the Winds is calling us, Tyler. Plus, I read that we'll be allowed to walk up to the base of Bridal Veil Falls. How about that?"

"Yes, Max, we can get tickets, but let's dry off first. Next, I want to take the Scenic Trolley through Niagara Park for a little relaxation."

"I'm with you; we have plenty of time for Caves. I'm up for the trolley ride—Niagara Park is remarkable, but I still want to see Rainbow Bridge."

Tyler smiles and replies, "In due time, Max."

CROSSING RAINBOW BRIDGE

"Tyler, to get into Canada, we need to cross the Niagara Falls International Rainbow Bridge. I looked it up. Now let me impress you. It's known as the Rainbow Bridge, an arch bridge across the Niagara River gorge. It connects the cities of Niagara Falls, New York, and Niagara Falls, Canada."

"I like your unbridled curiosity."

"Tyler, can we walk across Rainbow Bridge?"

"Yes, and we will, with our passports."

Max chuckles, "Horseshoe Falls, here we come."

"OK, first things first. We have to find the sign Leroy told us about."

"What sign, Tyler?"

"The one that tells us where to cross the bridge into Canada."

They walked briskly through the park. Max saw the sign; **Rainbow Bridge—Pedestrians Crossing to Canada.**

"I see it. Just think, Tyler, when we cross the bridge, we'll be in another country—Canada!"

"Are you up for it, Max?"

"You bet I am."

"Let's go for it."

It's a warm sunny afternoon, and a gentle breeze sifts across the bridge. Two teenagers tarry ahead of them. Tyler and Max take the cue and move at a leisurely pace. The opportunity presents itself, plenty of time to stop and take in the incredible surroundings.

"Tyler, I'd like to take a look at the Falls, but it's scary up here."

"Like always, take a deep breath. Come closer to my side. I'm right next to you. Don't look down, only look back. It's daunting, but at the same time, exhilarating."

Max turns his head slowly and glances over his shoulder.

"Tyler, I can't even think of words to describe the view."

"You know, Max, I'm rarely at a loss for words, but none would give justice to this sight and this moment."

The view of Niagara Falls from the Rainbow Bridge was gripping. At the midpoint on the bridge fence, a bronze plaque indicates the United States-Canada Boundary Line. Tyler and Max know it's significant.

Canada Border Services is ahead. Tyler and Max are next in line. An officer waves to come to his station, where he asks a few questions and examines their I.D. He smiles, returns their passports, and welcomes them into Canada.

Once in Canada, they spend the afternoon exploring local eateries and venues. Time passed quickly; the sun was setting. Tyler and Max got in line with other sightseers to view the nightly illumination of Niagara Falls.

Classical music was playing over the loudspeakers. When the lights flooded on, a handsome fellow and a black-furred beauty signaled them from across the rail. Tyler signaled back.

The duo made their way over. She was well coiffured and was sporting a red fedora with a brown feather. He was wearing a slate gray leather vest, a noticeably attractive couple.

"Hi, I'm Tyler, and Max is my brother. We're tourists from New York City, and we've come over to see the magical light show."

"My name is Justin, and Emmy is my girlfriend. You came to the right place. Now that they're on, what do you think?"

"Everyone should experience the show-stopping light show at Niagara Falls once in their lifetime. Completely engrossing and riveting!"

Enthralled by the brilliant color-changing lights' extravaganza, Max immerses himself in the fantasy.

Tyler inquires, "Justin, do you live in Canada, or are you on vacation, like us?"

"Niagara Falls is home. We're from Toronto, but we moved here last year."

"I see why it's such a vibrant city."

"We enjoy the nightlife. By the way, do you and Max have a place to stay for the night? If you don't, there's an empty drey two blocks away, past Clifton Hill. Last week, the group who lived there moved to Montreal."

"We'd like that. We're staying at the Niagara drey, but it's getting late. We'll check it out and most likely stay overnight."

"Look for the Maple Leaf drey, inside a massive maple tree in the back of Pens and Arrows gift shop. Turn right when you reach Clifton Hill. You can't miss it."

"Thanks, Justin."

"No problem. We're going home now. Emmy has to get up early. She has a radio show—*Mornings with Emmy,* at six in the morning, on Niagara Falls Talk radio station. It's always a pleasure to chat with tourists. Enjoy the rest of your visit."

"We will. Good night and thanks again, Justin and Emmy."

Whispering in Tyler's ear, "I kind of figured Emmy was some kind of celebrity. I think Justin is in show business. Maybe a model or an actor? Their flashy wardrobe and the way they look and carry themselves get a lot of attention."

"I thought so too, Max. If we're up at six, we can listen to her show. Another thing, I wouldn't mind having a vest like the one Justin was wearing."

"I can see you in it, and of course, you'll have Justin's swagger!"

"I don't know about that, Max. Now, let's see if we can find the Maple Leaf drey."

"Can we first make a stop at the gift shop Justin was telling us about?"

"Souvenir time?"

"Postcards, at least."

Climbing up to Clifton Hill toward Victoria Street, Pens and Arrows was in view.

Extensive shelves of statues and miniature Niagara Falls landmarks greet them. A revolving postcard card stand attracts Max.

After turning the stand several times, Max calls out, "I found the perfect card, Tyler! Look at this one! Don't you think it captures the spirit of the light show we just saw?"

"I would say so—fine selection."

"Let's buy three. We can send one to Aunt Julie and one to Teddy. The third will be for our wall."

"Let's check out now. We can buy some stamps too."

"I brought a few stamps from home."

"You know, Max, if we mail them in Canada, we'll need their stamps, not ours."

"I never thought of that, Tyler."

"Well, each country has its own postage system and stamps."

"Good to know."

After buying the postcards and stamps, Maple Leaf drey is next. Tyler spots an empty picnic table in a nearby park. They sit on the bench and write their postcards.

"Tyler, when Aunt Julie and Teddy get the postcards, I'm sure they'll want to see the beguiling theater of lights."

"Anyone who sees the postcard would."

They pass by a mailbox in front of an all-night pizza shop and mail the cards. An imposing maple tree with thick, sturdy branches is behind the gift shop. Tyler and Max crawl up. The Maple Leaf drey was spacious and comfortable. It couldn't have been too long ago that a vibrant community called it home. Someone left a lavender air freshener, which was still attached to a corner wall.

Tyler and Max curl up in a corner and banter about the exploits of the day. Time passes quickly, the discussion fades, and sleep takes over.

The drey was very dark; it was hard to determine if the sun was out. Tyler reached for his cell phone and looked at the time.

"Max, we have to get up. It's 10 a.m. already."

Rubbing his eyes and yawning, he answers, "Food, and then Caves!"

"We'll stop and get some breakfast sandwiches and coffee. Then we can head over to Rainbow Bridge."

"What about quarters, Tyler? Yesterday, I saw a sign in a store that said we'd each need one dollar in American or Canadian quarters when we cross back over."

"I almost forgot. Thanks for remembering. I have a few dollars tucked away. When we buy breakfast, I'll make sure to get eight quarters."

After breakfast, they make their way to Rainbow Bridge. The walk is invigorating. Passports and quarters are in hand. They notice a sign saying that pedestrians can now use credit cards or dollar bills for payment. Tyler and Max use their quarters to pay the toll. Getting back into the American side is a breeze. After checking passports and taking the fee, the agent welcomes Tyler and Max back home.

NEXT?

As they make their way back to Niagara drey, Leroy is outside taking in the sun. Max waves to him.

"How is your vacation so far, Max?"

"Couldn't be any better, yesterday we rode on Maid of the Mist and saw the grandeur and power of the Falls on display. Last night, we saw the light show—Niagara Falls illuminated in radiant colors."

"Yes, Max, that stunning vista is a must for all visitors. It's a nightly event."

"Leroy, we enjoyed Canada so much that we spent the night there."

"Glad to hear you were able to accomplish so many things."

"Leroy, I have a question for you. Captain Drake, our captain on the flight here, asked us if we were going to Anchor Bar. Is that a place we should visit?"

"My dear visitors, let me give you a few facts about the restaurant—then you decide if you want to go there."

Both sat up and paid attention. Leroy typed in Anchor Bar on his cell phone and read the narrative.

"In March, 1964, Dominic Bellissimo was tending bar at the now-famous Anchor Bar Restaurant here in Buffalo. One evening, a group of Dominic's friends arrived at the bar with ravenous appetites. Dominic asked his mother, Teressa, to prepare something for his friends to eat.

What she prepared, looked like chicken wings, a part of the chicken that usually went into the stock pot for soup. Teressa had deep fried the wings and flavored them with a secret sauce. The wings were an instant hit and it didn't take long for people to flock to the bar to experience their new taste sensation. From that evening on, *Buffalo wings* became a regular part of the menu at the Anchor Bar.

The phenomenon created in 1964 by Teressa Bellissimo has spread across the globe. Although many have tried to duplicate the Buffalo wing, the closely guarded secret recipe is what makes Frank & Teressa's the proclaimed *'Best Wings in the World'*."

Tyler and Max know why Captain Drake mentioned Anchor Bar. After hearing what Leroy read, how could anyone visit Buffalo and not go there?

"So, have I made a case for an outing to Anchor Bar, the birthplace of the world-renowned Buffalo chicken wings?"

Max asks, "Leroy, when are we going?"

"Tonight, around seven o'clock. You can meet me in front of the Scenic Trolley, at six-thirty. We'll take an Uber. I'll call Anchor Bar and make reservations."

"Liam, Max, and I will explore a few more attractions. But, at six-thirty sharp, we'll be waiting at the Scenic Trolley."

"See you then."

CAVE OF THE WINDS

Sunny weather, 85 degrees—set the stage to explore Cave of the Winds. Tyler and Max stood in line and bought two tickets. The agent gave them sandals and two ponchos.

"Here we go again, Tyler, another poncho. And a pair of sandals to help us walk along the slippery pathways. The worker introduced himself as Lee and said we could keep the sandals as a souvenir."

"I like reminders of our exploits."

"Let's just put on the plastic wrap and sandals and take the elevator. Lee told us we'd reach a short tunnel, which leads to the start of the wooden pathways. Our goal is to get to Hurricane Deck—feet from the Falls' plummeting water."

The initial set of stairs was manageable. As they climbed higher, the wind's intensity and pounding water increased dramatically. Each additional set of stairways became more difficult. They firmly gripped the wooden rails while being pelted with an intense and un-yielding water spray and tried to hang on. It became evident that perhaps the Caves and the explosive sheets of rain were a bit too much.

"Can't stop the splashing water. It just keeps coming at me. I don't know about this, Tyler!"

"Well, Max, you were all gung ho about Caves. We're going to get through this. I'm right behind you. Climb slowly. We have quite a few staircases ahead of us before reaching the top. Always know where your feet are. Hold on to the rails. You'll be fine!"

Slippery paths and blasting water seemed like a mini-typhoon. Determination and an unrelenting spirit bolstered them to the zenith—Hurricane Deck, where a thick mist glazed the wooden frames. Pint-sized buckets of water cascaded and thrashed around them. Minutes seemed like hours.

As he tried to open his water-logged eyes, Max shouted, "We made it, Tyler, we made it!"

With arms outstretched and vitality regained, he proclaims, "Indeed, we did, Max! We persevered, and here we are!"

Though thoroughly drenched, the thundering sound and visual imagery entertained their senses.

"I don't know how long we've been up here, Max. What an electrifying experience!"

"Tyler, it was frightening, but I had you to help me. Cousin Teddy always says to trust yourself when faced with any difficulty. Between you and Teddy, I couldn't go wrong. I learned I have to gather my inner strength when dealing with adversity."

"Very well said, Max."

Going down the steps seemed a lot easier than the climb up. At the bottom, there was a receptacle to discard ponchos. Towels were available. They dried off the best they could. It was over 85 degrees; the slight dampness was welcome. It even felt good.

"Max, How about we head back to Niagara drey, relax, and then meet up with Leroy this evening?"

"I could use a little rest."

Off came the sunglasses when they entered the drey. Music was playing in the background. Both found a quiet corner and dozed.

9
ANCHOR BAR/BUFFALO WINGS

When they woke up, it was almost time to meet for dinner. Max donned his maroon beret, and Tyler put on his silver brocade waist belt. The Scenic Trolley was around the corner. Leroy was waiting and texted for an Uber; he looked quite dapper with his gold chain and paisley ascot.

In less than five minutes, a grey metallic Mercedes SUV pulled up. The driver came out of the car and introduced himself. He was wearing a black suit with a green plaid bow tie.

"My name is Carlton. I'll be your driver this evening. Be careful getting in. Please, let me know if there's any special music you'd like to hear on our ride over to 1047 Main Street, the Anchor Bar. I've taken many folks to that address. That's how I know it."

Leroy rode in the front seat. Tyler and Max sat in the back.

"All seat belts fastened?" Carlton asked as he drove away.

"Carlton, the back is all secured."

Leroy just nodded in the affirmative.

The ride was delightful. It smelled like a wintergreen forest, and soft music was playing. After a short ride, Anchor Bar was in view.

Getting out of the Uber, all thanked Carlton for a safe ride.

Looking up at the restaurant, Leroy proclaims, "There's a lot of history here. I'll give you some fun tidbits."

"Max enjoys learning the local minutia first hand, Tyler chants in."

"How about we get seated first?"

"Whatever you say, Leroy. Tyler and I are honored to be here."

Leroy chooses a corner table surrounded by overhead motorcycles and artwork. Loud music is playing in the background. Customers are moving about and gazing at the memorabilia.

A server brings three glasses of ice water to the table and hands them menus.

"Hello, my name is Marcie. I'll be back in a few to take your order.

If you have any questions, just let me know."

"Let's look at the menu, and I'll answer your questions. Stan and I eat here quite often. You can imagine that any time we have guests, first on the list—Anchor Bar."

"By the way, where is Stan tonight? He didn't want to come with us?" inquired Tyler.

"It's not that he didn't want to, Tyler. A girlfriend from Binghamton came to visit unexpectedly."

"I understand. Maybe they'll be here later."

Max examines the menu and observes excitedly, "Tyler, see what I see?"

"You mean, all the types of wings?"

"That, yes, but here's the story about Teressa Bellissimo. Right here on the top of the menu. It's what you read to us, Leroy."

"Sure is. Anchor Bar is quite an icon. It made its mark on the world with Buffalo chicken wings."

"Quite an extensive menu with so many choices. I like Anchor Bar's vibrancy, and with the enticing aroma filling the restaurant, I'm getting hungry. I'm ready to order Leroy. What do you recommend?"

"Buffalo wings, certainly. The spicier, the better for me. I don't know if that's down your alley?"

"Tyler likes spicy. I'd prefer something tamer."

"My suggestion, an order of hot spicy wings and an order of mild."

"THE REAL STORY"

On March 4th, 1964, Dominic Bellissimo was tending bar at the now famous Anchor Bar Restaurant in Buffalo, NY. Late that evening, a group of Dominic's friends arrived at the bar with ravenous appetites. Dominic asked his mother, Teressa, to prepare something for his friends to eat. They looked like chicken wings, a part of the chicken that usually went into the stock pot for soup.

Teressa had deep fried the wings and flavored them with a secret sauce. The wings were an instant hit and it didn't take long for people to flock to the bar to experience this new taste sensation. From that evening on, Buffalo Wings became a regular part of the menu at the Anchor Bar.

The phenomenon created in 1964 by Teressa Bellissimo has spread across the globe. Although many have tried to duplicate Buffalo Wings, the closely guarded secret recipe is what makes Frank & Teressa's the proclaimed "Best Wings in the World."

ORIGINAL ANCHOR BAR WING SOUP!
Ask your server.

Frank & Teressa's

ANCHOR® BAR

• BUFFALO ORIGINALS •

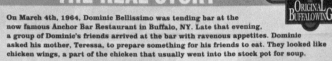

ANCHOR BAR'S WORLD FAMOUS WINGS

All of our world famous wing orders are served with traditional celery and bleu cheese, just like Mother served us that famous night in 1964. We want our loyal customers to know that we use only unsaturated zero gram trans fat to fry our wings.

Bleu cheese & ranch dressing $1.00 each

🐔 MILD, MEDIUM, HOT, SPICY HOT BBQ, CHIPOTLE BBQ, SPICY GARLIC PARMESAN

Single (10) $13.00
Double (20) $21.00
Bucket (50) $48.00
Only doubles & buckets can be split into two flavors.

🐔 SUICIDAL `IF YOU DARE!` EXTREME HEAT!

Single (10) $14.00
Double (20) $22.00
Bucket (50) $48.00
Only doubles & buckets can be split into two flavors.

RUBS
Cool Habanero & Original Buffalo

WINGS THAT FLY
WE SHIP our wings all over the country! Ask your server for more information! or visit: www.anchorbar.com

---

TRADITIONAL ANCHOR BAR STYLE! # PIZZA **ADDITIONAL TOPPINGS** sm $2.00 | lg $2.30

Onions · Sausage · Mushrooms · Green Olives · Black Olives · Hot Peppers · Green Peppers · Bacon · Pepperoni

CHEESE & PEPPERONI......................sm $12.00 | lg $15.00

WHITE PIZZA ....sm $14.00 | lg $17.00
Olive oil, chopped onion, tomato, parmesan cheese and mozzarella cheese

🐔 : ANCHOR BAR SIGNATURE ITEMS

Marcie, the attractive blonde waitress, was standing with her notepad, ready to take the order.

"My buddies and I have decided on two orders of Buffalo wings."

"How would you like those prepared, and what size?"

"Marcie, Let's try one order of hot, make that extra-large. And one mild, medium size"

"You got it."

"Thank you."

"Now, what about the décor, all the bikes, Leroy?"

"The motorcycles decorating the interior are like nothing you've ever seen. There are old bikes and some newer models. The worn-out signs tell the make, model, and year. Most belonged to a former owner, who left them for all customers to admire and enjoy. Awesome, don't you think so, Max?"

"Awesome, indeed! Yes, amusing. Tell us some more."

"Well, for years, live music, mostly jazz, has played here, and the tradition continues. Patrons can enjoy the Buffalo wings and other delicacies while listening to local talent."

The scrumptious Buffalo wings made it to their table. Tyler and Max didn't expect the celery sticks and blue cheese dressing. Leroy picked up on their not knowing how to start and stepped in.

"Tyler, Max, dig in. Dip the wings in the dressing and chomp on the celery sticks. The combination works well. You can put any bones in the little brown bowls."

Max thinks for a few minutes, then follows Leroy's advice.

Before anyone starts eating, Max blurts out, "*Bon appétit*! I learned that French phrase from a cousin back home."

Leroy smiles and respectfully replies, "*Bon appétit!*"

Tyler and Leroy reach for the spicy, while Max enjoys the mild. No one talks until all the wings and fixings are gone.

Empty plates and water glasses were all that was left. Hand wipes were available for the final clean-up.

"Leroy, how can we ever thank you for your time and goodwill? You offered us your drey and gave us advice on the tourist sites. You introduced us to the top-notch Anchor Bar. We'll always remember its *avant-garde* ambiance and walled motorcycles."

"It has been my pleasure, Tyler. I know what it's like to be by yourself in a new town. I live in an extraordinary city, but in reality, I live quite an ordinary life. You and Max broke up my daily routine for the better. Anchor Bar is a treat for me too."

"Leroy, Max, and I would like the meal to be on us."

"Heavens no, besides, I already paid the bill and left a generous tip for Marcie. When I get to Forest Hills, you can treat me to a New York delicacy."

"Agreed."

Max adds, "You've been our advocate. You showed us Niagara Falls from a native's perspective. And we will never forget Anchor Bar."

"I truly enjoyed your visit and was happy to make your vacation memorable."

"Gentlemen, since you're leaving early in the morning, I think it's high time we head back to Niagara Falls. I'll call an Uber. Why don't you pick out a few Anchor Bar souvenirs and have them shipped to Forest Hills."

"Great idea. Max, let's go look at the display."

"Oh, yes."

"What do you think of the Anchor Bar Flying Buffalo? I think we could hang it on the room divider."

"Let's get two, Max, one for your side and one for mine."

"Let's not forget Aunt Julie and Cousin Teddy."

"That's right."

"I think an Anchor Bar Chicken Key Chain for Teddy and an Anchor Bar Coffee Mug for Aunt Julie."

"I like your selections, Max. Give our address to the cashier and pay with Aunt Julie's credit card. I'll go outside and wait with Leroy."

Just in the nick of time, Max comes out with the credit card receipt. A navy Jeep Grand Cherokee is entering the driveway.

The driver greets them and asks for a name.

"I'm Leroy, and I requested a ride to Niagara Falls."

"That's what I have on my tablet, Mr. Leroy."

"My name is Ray. It will be a quick ride back, not much traffic this evening."

Ray opened the back door and let Tyler and Max in. Leroy sat up front. When they reached Niagara Falls, Ray had to wake everyone up.

Leroy thanked Ray. Tyler and Max followed Leroy back to the drey.

In the hallway, Leroy spoke quietly, "I'll be sleeping when you leave, so I want to say goodbye and good luck with your trip back to New York City."

"Good night, Leroy, and thanks again for all your insights and guidance. Max and I have the memories of a lifetime, and we won't make a sound in the morning."

Smiles are exchanged.

10
ON OUR WAY HOME

It was peaceful, and fresh floral air was flowing into the Niagara drey.

"Max, it's already five-thirty."

"I'm up. Stan left us a note—it says to have a safe trip back to Forest Hills. He left us a bag of goodies. The bus leaves at six o'clock, from Niagara Theater."

"Do we have everything in our backpack?"

"Tyler, I think so. I packed our sunglasses. We hardly need them. It is pitch black outside. I will wear my beret, though. I folded our roll-up pillows, the ones Aunt Julie gave us to use on our trip. Easy to pack and served us well. We can use them on the train."

"Sounds good. We'll need them. I'll pack the bag from Stan. I don't know how much longer I can keep my eyes open."

NYC BOUND

With their backpacks firmly secured and tickets to New York Penn Station readily available in the outer pocket, they wait at Niagara Adventure Theater. A grey bus pulls up, with the sign above the driver's window—**Niagara Falls AMTRAK.**

The front door opens, and the driver announces loudly, "Bus to Niagara Falls Amtrak Station—all aboard."

Two young girls with small carry-on bags boarded. Tyler and Max followed. Three more passengers with large suitcases came on.

At 6 a.m., a recorded announcement was made.

Niagara Falls Amtrak next stop. Please make sure your seatbelts are fastened. No smoking allowed. Thank you for your cooperation.

The front door closed, the inside lights dimmed, and the bus started moving.

The ride was uneventful, it was dark, and there wasn't much to see. In less than 30 minutes, the bus was turning into Niagara Falls Amtrak Station's driveway.

The station was open for business. Once inside, Tyler showed the attendant their tickets and inquired if they needed anything else.

"No, you are all set, and thank you for choosing Amtrak Empire Service."

The sun was rising; most passengers went outside and waited for the 7:50 a.m. to New York City.

At 7:45 a.m., a shiny Amtrak Empire Service train pulled into the station, which is the only train line that connects Niagara Falls to New York City.

Tyler and Max follow the crowd to the train platform. The conductor opens the front door and invites everyone to board the train to Penn Station, with a stop in Buffalo.

"Tyler, I didn't know we were going to make a stop in Buffalo?" Do you think we'll have to change trains?"

"I don't know, Max, we'll ask, but let's get our seats."

The two shuffle to the second car and take seats near the snack bar.

"Remember, Tyler, we have nuts, fruit, and some local Buffalo treat from Stan. I peeked in the bag before we left."

"I just want to sleep, Max. Let's get our pillows and have them ready. We'll wait for the conductor to take our tickets, then we can grab a few winks."

A final announcement is made for all passengers to board. A few stragglers get on at the last minute. As they take their seats, the train moves slowly from Niagara Falls Station. It's 7:50 a.m., right on time.

A recorded PA announcement is made.

Good morning and welcome aboard **Amtrak Empire Service** to New York City, Penn Station. There will be one stop in Buffalo-Depew. A conductor will be coming through shortly to collect tickets. Please have them available.

There are lavatories and a cafe bar for your convenience. If there is anything you need, just let one of the staff members know. Thank you for your attention, and welcome aboard.

The train moves at a well-clipped pace. A conductor in a navy blue uniform is collecting tickets and answering questions.

"Tickets, please."

Max hands her the tickets.

"Thank you; I see you're going all the way to Penn Station."

"Yes, we are. Do we have a long stop in Buffalo?"

"No, we'll pick up more passengers and be on our way in less than 30 minutes."

"Thank you. May I ask a question?"

"Sure, what would you like to know?"

"I like your uniform, but what do those navy patches mean?"

"The ones on my shoulders?"

"Yes."

"They are epaulets and color-coded to reflect specific job functions. I'm an assistant conductor, so I wear navy blue epaulets. When I get promoted, hopefully, next month, the epaulets change to navy blue with teal stripes."

"I like them; you look very professional. By the way, I'm Max, and sleeping next to me is my brother Tyler."

"Very nice to meet you, Max, my name is Tina. If you need anything, I'm here to assist you."

"Thanks, Tina."

"You're welcome, and enjoy the ride."

Max was looking around and observing the goings-on in the cabin. A strong coffee aroma filled the air. The woman across the aisle had a cup of tea and what looked like two bite-sized glazed donuts. A man in a beige suit was reading the *Wall Street Journal*.

Thoughts turned to Leroy and Stan. A hope was that he and Tyler could return the hospitality the two had afforded them. He thought of taking the guests to Central Park. Scenarios swirled through his mind. Buffalo chicken wings and seeing all the hanging motorcycles was quite an experience. What a fond memory; the evening with Leroy at the Anchor Bar.

Everyone sat up and paid attention when the following announcement came over the loudspeaker.

"May I have your attention? The next stop, coming up very shortly, will be Buffalo-Depew. If that is your stop, please take the time to look above and around your seat and gather your personal belongings. When the train stops, make your way to the nearest exit where you see a uniformed crew member, as not all doors will open.

If you're continuing to Penn Station and decide to get off the train, make sure you have your ticket with you. The train to Penn Station will depart at 9:30 a.m. Please watch your step when exiting the train, and thank you for choosing Amtrak."

"Tyler, wake up! Did you hear that? We're already in Buffalo."

About 15 passengers got off in Buffalo. Uniformed crew members were coming through to tidy the cabin.

"Tyler, I'd like to see the Buffalo-Depew station."

"Yes, we could use a little exercise."

They got off the train. While walking around, a bison statue caught their eye. Max went over to see it.

"Tyler, come here and look at the magnificent bison. I want a photo."

He took his cell phone from his waistband and selected the camera feature. He focused on the bison and told him, "Smile and say cheese."

"Max, the bison statue isn't going to smile, and it's certainly not going to say anything—especially cheese."

"I know, but I thought it was funny. The placard says that the statue was dedicated on the lawn in front of the depot, on September 23, 2014."

"You've taken quite a few pictures on our trip; I can't wait to see them, Max."

A loud announcement is made:

"Amtrak for Penn Station will depart in 10 minutes. All aboard!"

Just as Tina had told them—only 30 minutes at Buffalo-Depew, at 9:15 a.m., passengers began boarding.

Tyler and Max climb the steps and return to their seats. They listen to the announcement.

"Penn Station, New York City, is the next and final stop."

Everyone buckles up as the train rolls steadily down the track, away from the station. Tina and another conductor start collecting tickets.

Tyler adjusts his seat and sinks into his pillow. Most passengers have fallen asleep, but Max is wide awake and gazes out the window. He is fascinated by the passing scenery. Extensive green pastures have plenty of freshly milked cows grazing in the morning sun. Factory workers were pulling into parking lots, ready to begin the workday.

Passing the Finger Lakes reminded him of how much water graces New York State. All the sights amuse him; there are animals he has never seen, and he takes it all in.

Near Albany, Tyler wakes up. He reaches for his water bottle and takes a few sips.

Rubbing his eyes and trying to focus, Tyler asks, "What about the treats Stan gave us?"

"There's walnuts and figs. I had a few figs, ripe and sweet. Now, I'm enjoying a piece of sponge candy."

"Sponge candy, what's that?"

"It's a local specialty, from *Watson's*. Look, *Watson's* is printed on the ribbon tied around the package. Do you want some? It's yummy."

"Yes, Max, I'd like to try some sponge candy."

"OK, you'll enjoy it, crispy and tasty."

Tyler takes a piece of dark chocolate sponge. After chewing on it slowly, he smiles.

"Yes, crispy, and a caramel flavor. Nice combination."

"Changing the subject, Tyler, you won't believe what I saw when you were napping."

He excitedly rambles on, exclaiming, "Cows—big ones and small ones. I saw a bunch of girls riding horses around a lake. The colors were unusual, like someone had taken a brush and painted each horse. The sign said—Finger Lake region. There was a field of spinning windmills perched on top of lush rolling hills. New York State is huge, Tyler. Lots of greenery and gas stations."

"I'm awake now; I'll be able to see what's happening outside. I'd like to see some real cows. I've only seen pictures in books. Hopefully, more horses will be romping around."

Barely hearing anything, Max puts his head on the pillow and finds a comfortable resting position. It was now Tyler's turn to see what so impressed his brother.

He saw three deer racing through a valley and finally got to see real cows. With over 25 black and white cows, an enormous pasture was in view. Tyler knew the next few hours would be his time to put everything in perspective. Quietly thinking, the outdoor visuals relax his spirit.

Tyler and Max are adrift in their dreams until a loud voice interrupts their peace.

"May I have your attention? The next and final stop will be Penn Station, New York City, coming up shortly. Please take this time to look above and around your seat and gather your personal belongings. When the train stops, make your way to the nearest exit where you see a uniformed crew member, as not all doors will open. Thank you for choosing Amtrak. Enjoy the rest of your day."

At 4 p.m., the Amtrak from Niagara Falls and Buffalo arrived. Everyone listened to the welcoming announcement and gathered their belongings. Tyler and Max thanked Tina, who was at the exit door, for her excellent service. She smiled and thanked them for riding Amtrak.

BACK TO FOREST HILLS

Max looks around Penn Station and takes out his cell phone.

"Tyler, I want to take a photo of Penn."

"Go ahead. I'll text for our ride."

Max shows it to Tyler.

"Very symbolic. We'll get it made into a hanging picture. Max, can you see it displayed on the wall divider in our drey?"

Smiling confidently, "Yes, I can. Penn Station is the finale of our enthralling and enjoyable venture. That must count for something!"

The ride to their humble abode was the culmination of a well-planned sojourn. It was a joy to be home.

GERALDINE FERRARO WAY

"You know, Tyler, we're home, and I'm dead tired, but I have one last question about Austin Street."

"Yes, Austin was the first street we crossed."

"Did you ever notice that written below Austin Street is Geraldine Ferraro Way? Why would a street have two names?"

"Let me tell you. When a person's name is affixed to a street sign, that particular person was probably from the area and somehow made a notable contribution. Ms. Ferraro was a resident of Forest Hills Gardens. In 1984, she was the Democratic Party choice for vice president of the United States."

"Did Ferraro win the election?"

"No. Afterwards, she returned to Congress. See how appropriate the co-name Geraldine Ferraro Way fits with Austin Street?"

"Even more history in our area Tyler. What street did she live on?"

"Deepdene Road, a tranquil, hidden-away area in Forest Hills Gardens."

"Add Deepdene Road to our list of places to visit."

"For sure, later, when we're rested."

The two use all the energy they can muster and very slowly climb to their drey.

When Max reaches the first branch, he looks up to the sky.

"Tyler, see the moon? It's a full moon."

"Wow, and it's lighting up the whole sky!"

"Tyler, I think it means good luck."

"We've been pretty lucky so far."

"We have. You are right. It might be too early to start a bucket list at our age, Tyler. Think about it, though. We've already been on an airplane, taken a train ride, and visited another country."

"Max, I assure you, the best is yet to come!"

The phone rings as soon as they enter their tranquil dwelling. Max answers.

"Hello."

"Good evening, I'm Otis Parson, and I would like to speak with Tyler or Max."

"Yes, Mr. Parson, this is Max."

"You may remember me from Paley Park?"

"Yes, I do. It was a cool spring day."

"I'm calling to see if you and your brother are agreeable to come to my studio in Manhattan for a photoshoot."

"That sounds great, Mr. Parson. We were waiting for your call."

"I know it's late. I'll have Della call you tomorrow to schedule an appointment. She'll tell you everything you'll need to bring."

"Thank you, Mr. Parson. Tyler and I will be waiting for her call."

Max jumps up and down, "Tyler, I'm so tired, but now I won't be able to sleep."

Tyler doesn't answer. He's in dreamland. Fast asleep on the pillow, he dug out of his backpack.

Whispering, even though he knows Tyler can't hear, "Everything is within our grasp, Tyler—everything!"

PHOTO GALLERY

Deep in the North Woods,

a split in the path appeared.

"Which way now, Liam?"

"Let's continue straight ahead."

Tyler then whispers to Max,

"Next time, we will take the left."

—Gwyn Dunham